Text copyright © Paul Bright 2009 • Illustrations copyright © Lee Wildish 2009
Original edition published in English by Little Tiger Press, an imprint of
Magi Publications, London, England, 2009 • LTP/1400/0111/0610 • Printed in China
Library of Congress Cataloging-in-Publication Data
Bright, Paul. • Charlie's superhero underpants / Paul Bright;
[illustrations] Lee Wildish. • p. cm. • Summary: When a gusting wind blows
the laundry off the clothesline, Charlie travels the world searching for his
favorite scarlet superhero underpants. • ISBN 978-1-56148-679-3
(hardcover : alk. paper) [1. Stories in rhyme. 2. Underwear--Fiction.
3. Voyages and travels--Fiction.] I. Wildish, Lee, ill. II. Title.
PZ8.3.B7675Ch 2010 • [E]--dc22 • 2009031142

For Katie, with love ~ P B

For Laura, Grace and Oscar ~ L W

Paul Bright

Lee Wildish

CHARLIE'S SUPERHERO UNDERPANTS

Good Books

Intercourse, PA 17534
800/762-7171
www.GoodBooks.com

On a wild and windy day,
around about the end of May,
A great and gusting gale
blew the laundry clean away.

Socks and shirts, a woolly hat,
but far worse than all of that,
Was Young Charlie's Superhero Underpants.

PO W!

As it soared into the sky,
the laundry billowed, flapped and swirled,
Until it scattered far and wide,
to all the corners of the world.

Though they searched
for days and nights,
and planes and satellites,
with boats

They found **no trace** of
Charlie's Underpants.

They had **POW!**
across the front,
in giant letters,
bold and black,

With KERZAP! and OOF!
and SPLAT! a little smaller
on the back.

And villains would take fright
as Charlie pulled his pants up tight,
His Scarlet Superhero
Underpants.

Charlie packed
some sandwiches,
some sardines
and some soap,

A mirror, fan and toothbrush,
and a big brass telescope.

"Don't worry and don't wait," he said.
"I may be back quite late.
But I've got to find my
Scarlet Underpants."

First Charlie grabbed a ride
with a band in a balloon,
And they crossed the choppy Channel
to a bouncy, brassy tune.

There they spied
a fine French fox,
wearing sister Sophie's socks,
But they saw no sign of Charlie's Underpants.

Angleterre

Culotte

Charlie hiked across
the endless plain of Serengeti,
Where the insects made him itchy
and the sunshine made him sweaty.

And there he saw a lion,
with a stripy shirt and tie on,
But no Scarlet Superhero Underpants.

Charlie climbed and clambered
up the plateau of Peru,
Where the breeze that blows at night
makes you shiver through and through.

And he found
a pair of llamas
wearing brother Ben's pajamas,

But he couldn't find his
Scarlet Underpants.

Charlie searched the length
of the mighty Mississippi,
Though the Mississippi's muddy
and the mud's all soft and slippy.

And an **alligator** sat,
wearing Grandpa's woolly hat,
But it wasn't wearing Charlie's Underpants.

Charlie was fed up.
He felt lonely, tired and small,
On a steep and snowy hillside
in the mountains of Nepal.

When suddenly he saw,
in that land of ice and cold,
A huge and hairy creature,
something wondrous to behold.

Charlie blinked and rubbed his eyes.
It couldn't be . . .

it could . . .

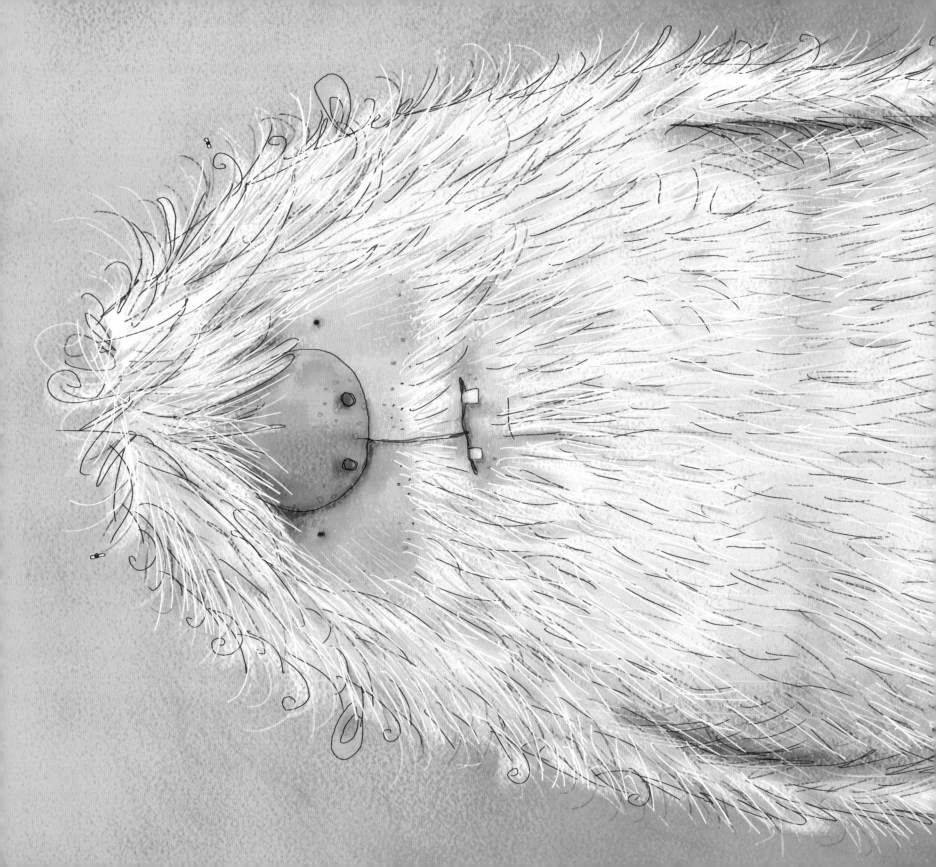

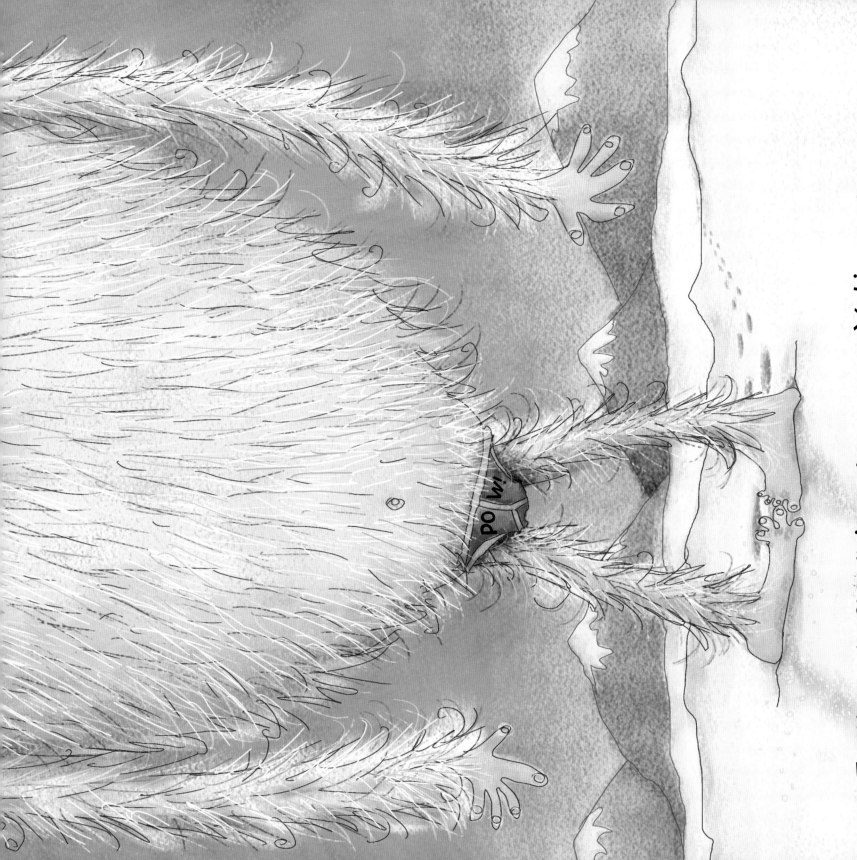

For there, in Charlie's Underpants, a Yeti proudly stood.

"My Underpants!" cried Charlie. "They're the ones I love the most."

"But they're mine now," growled the Yeti. "And they keep me warm as toast!"

"I'll swap you," Charlie said.
"You'll be snug from toes to head,
If you'll give me back my Scarlet Underpants."

Charlie thanked the Yeti
and he pulled his pants up tight.
They had POW! across the front,
so he had put them on just right.

He raised one arm up high, and he flew into the sky . . .

In his Scarlet Superhero

Underpants!